# Little Angel
## comes to stay

Rachel Anderson

Illustrated by Linda Birch

Oxford University Press

Oxford Melbourne Toronto

Oxford University Press, Walton Street, Oxford OX2 6DP

Oxford   London   Glasgow
New York   Toronto   Melbourne   Auckland
Kuala Lumpur   Singapore   Hong Kong   Tokyo
Delhi   Bombay   Calcutta   Madras   Karachi
Nairobi   Dar es Salaam   Cape Town

and associated companies in
Beirut   Berlin   Ibadan   Mexico City   Nicosia

*Oxford* is a trade mark of Oxford University Press

© Rachel Anderson 1984

First published 1984

ISBN 0 19 271472 4

British Library Cataloguing in Publication Data

Anderson Rachel
Little angel comes to stay.
I. Title        *
823'.914[J]   PZ7

ISBN 0 19 271472 4

Typeset by Wyvern Typesetting Ltd, Bristol
Printed in Hong Kong

## Chapter 1

'But *why* are you going out *tonight*?' Gabrielle screamed at her mother. She already knew why, for her parents often had to go out, and she always screamed about it. 'Why must I be left alone with that woman?'

'Because we're going out to dinner, poppet. And then we shall play bridge. Now eat up your supper, sweetie.' Gabrielle's mother admired her new curly hairstyle in the mirror. 'Mrs Brown's a very capable person, and a nice reliable babysitter. If you feel lonely, she can chat to you.'

'I don't want an ancient old babysitter to chat to me,' said Gabrielle. She pushed aside her chocolate-chip ice-cream and her fruit salad, and she pushed out her lower lip. 'I want somebody my own age to chat to.' Then she pulled the bowl back and stirred the ice-cream into a brown puddle.

'Yes, petkins,' said Gabrielle's mother. She patted her hair and tweaked at her evening dress.

'I wouldn't be so *lonely* going to bed on my own,' said Gabrielle, 'if I had a child here.'

'I'll ask Mrs Brown to let you stay up an extra half-hour,' said her mother. 'If she ever gets here! I hope she hasn't missed that bus again.'

'If I had a sister just my own age, and another sister a bit younger, and some brothers too, and a baby, then I wouldn't be lonely. I wish I was part of a *big* family with all different sized people in it,' Gabrielle said.

'Yes, popsie!' said her mother.

'And I wish we lived in town near the shops,' Gabrielle added because, while she was wishing for things, it seemed a good idea to get in as many as possible.

'Do eat up your nice fruit, and please try not to grate on my nerves with that horrid whine.'

'If you'd let me be part of a big family, I wouldn't have to be cross and grate on your nerves.'

Gabrielle's father ran downstairs, looking at his watch. He adjusted his bow-tie.

'Mildred!' he called. 'If we don't leave soon, we're going to arrive hours after everybody else.'

Gabrielle tipped her melted ice-cream into the sink, and cut herself a chunk of chocolate cake. 'If I was part of a big family,' she went on, 'I would play

Schools. And Mothers and Fathers. And Hide-and-Seek, just like they do in proper families. I'd teach them how to do sums on my calculator, and show them how to mix colours with my French Artist Set. I *want* to be part of a big family!'

She stamped her foot and glared at her mother. Usually when she did this while saying that she wanted something, within a week she had it. That way, she had come to own a toy typewriter, a cassette-player, a sequinned disco jumpsuit, a bedside radio-clock which lit up in the dark, and a white rabbit.

Mrs Brown, the babysitter, arrived in a flurry, and hung up her coat. Gabrielle's father strode out to start the car. Gabrielle's mother kissed Gabrielle goodnight, and hurried out as quickly as she could. Gabrielle heard the car door slam and the car drive away. She glared at Mrs Brown.

'Here we are then,' said Mrs Brown. 'Have you had all you want to eat, Gabby?' and she began to clear Gabrielle's supper things into the sink.

'Yes, and my name is not Gabby,' said Gabrielle and she pushed past Mrs Brown, put her portable television set on the windowsill, and turned up the volume as loud as it would go. She stood close to the screen, with her back to Mrs Brown, but she did not watch the programme.

'If I was part of a proper family, I wouldn't have to watch television. I could play Snakes and Ladders, and Ludo, and Cluedo, and Murder in the Dark.'

Mrs Brown glanced up. 'What is it, dear? Do you want to play a game?'

Gabrielle said nothing and clenched her teeth. There was no point in even trying to play a complicated board game with Mrs Brown, for Mrs Brown always forgot the rules as fast as you explained them.

## Chapter 2

'Tonight, precious,' said Gabrielle's mother, 'your father and I have to go to the opera. It's rather a special occasion.' She had a new evening dress, and another new hairdo with all her hair dyed red, and swept up into a mass of curls on top of her head. 'Your father has booked us a table for dinner afterwards.'

'So I suppose that person has to come and babysit me again!' said Gabrielle scowling.

'No. Wretched Mrs Brown. She's let us down at the last minute. And she always seemed such a *reliable* woman. The daughter can't come either, not at short notice. Anyway, we're going to be out so late. I've arranged a lovely surprise. You shall spend the night in town with our very dear friends the Potters.'

'But I don't know the Potters.'

'Yes you do, sweetie. We met them when you were little. You must have forgotten.'

'If I can't remember them, how *can* I know them?' said Gabrielle. She picked up her mother's false eyelashes and tried them on.

'Don't fiddle, Gabrielle honey. And please try not to be difficult about this evening.'

'I'm not,' said Gabrielle. 'I'm just saying I don't know them. I don't care who babysits me as long as it's not Mrs Brown again. I *hate* Mrs Brown babysitting me. How long have I got to stay with these people?'

'Just a fleeting visit, petkins. Your father and I will drop you off on our way to the opera house.' Gabrielle's mother began to pluck her eyebrows with a pair of tweezers.

'Will they like me? What will I do there? Will I be allowed to stay up late? Will Mrs Potter see me to bed, and read me my bedtime story, and cook me a nice supper and fold up my clothes for me?'

'I expect so, cherub. It'll be just like being here, except you'll be there. They're a lovely family. Now stop asking silly questions, angel, because you're beginning to grate again.'

'Are they a *proper* family?' asked Gabrielle.

'Gabrielle, will you please run along and play in

8

your treehouse while I finish getting ready. No, not your treehouse! You'll fall out. Play on your swing.'

'How many children are there? More than one?'

'Several. Please don't fiddle with my nail varnish.'

'More than three?'

'Yes, Gabrielle. I expect so.' Gabrielle's mother took her new evening dress out of her wardrobe.

'Good,' said Gabrielle. 'I am glad. I do hope they've got lots and lots and lots. Do they play Hide-and-Seek? And Hunt-the-Slipper? I wish I could stay there a long time, not just one night. Why can't I? I think I'd probably like to stay with the Potters for at least a week.' Gabrielle had stayed in four-star hotels in London, Paris, Rome and the *Costa del Sol*, but always with her parents. She had never before stayed anywhere on her own, especially with a big family who lived in town.

'Do they have a real pavement, right up to the front door? And street lamps outside, on all night?' she asked.

'I expect so. Now please will you find something to do, and let me have my nap?' Gabrielle's mother lay down on her bed and closed her eyes.

9

Gabrielle went to her own room. From her wardrobe she took her white vanity case with a red lining and brass hinges. Into it she packed her sequin jumpsuit in case they went to a disco, and her green velvet dress with a muslin collar in case they went to a party, and her blue silk dress in case they went out to tea. She packed her frilly pyjamas which her father had brought her from New York, and her yellow sponge-bag and matching yellow shower cap which her father had brought her from Paris.

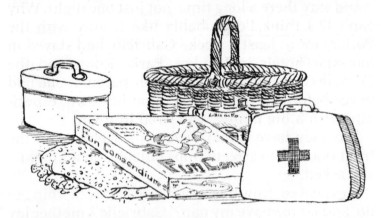

Then she went to her playroom and into a wicker basket she packed pencils and paper in case the Potters wanted to play noughts and crosses and consequences; and her compendium of Four Favourite Family Games so that she would be able to play Ludo, Snakes and Ladders, Dominoes and Blow Football. She packed her nurse's outfit and her Junior Red Cross kit so that she would be able to play Hospitals. She also packed her Stencilling Set, and her miniature sewing-machine, and her Make-a-Paper-Flower Kit, and her dolls' tea set, and a pack of cards, and some plasticine, and her pocket calculator, as well as several other useful things.

## Chapter 3

In readiness for the opera, Gabrielle's father came home from work early, and Gabrielle's mother put on her new long dress.

'You do look nice,' said Gabrielle. Her mother wore silver shoes, and carried a silver bag.

'Now, cherub, here's a strawberry gateau from the freezer for you to give to the Potters. I don't suppose they have strawberries very often. And have you

11

remembered your dressing-gown?'

'Which one?' asked Gabrielle, for she had two, a thin flowery one and a thick blue fluffy one which she liked even more.

'Take the warm one, for I don't believe the Potters keep their bedrooms heated.'

When Gabrielle's parents were ready to leave for the opera, they could not decide which of their cars to take. The silvery saloon, said Gabrielle's mother, would look better arriving at the opera house. On the other hand, said Gabrielle's father, if they didn't get a move on, by the time they'd dropped Gabrielle off, they would miss the first act altogether, so they'd better use the sports car.

Even though there was hardly any room for her on the narrow back seat—and today with the vanity case, the basket of useful things and the cake carton, even less room than usual—Gabrielle always preferred the sports car. Gabrielle's mother, however, was not so pleased about going in the sports car, because her new hairdo got squashed against the low roof, and her evening dress got shut in the door.

They pulled up outside the Potter's house. 'Are you *sure* this is right?' Gabrielle asked, for the houses in the terrace seemed taller and thinner than Gabrielle had imagined town houses should be.

'Yes, poppet. Hurry up. Don't want to keep your Papa waiting,' said Gabrielle's mother.

'Don't dawdle, Gabrielle,' said her father. 'You know we're in a hurry.'

Gabrielle's mother staggered out of the car, clutching her glittering skirts. Gabrielle followed with her case, her basket and the cake carton. Gabrielle's father drummed his fingers on the steering-wheel.

On the Potters' doorstep a cat sat washing itself. On the pavement a pram stood, filled with tins of food and a live baby. The baby was held by straps. As they passed near its pram, the baby half stood up, as far as the straps would allow it, and threw a tin of sardines onto the pavement.

The front door was open wide, so that Gabrielle could see into the hall and halfway up the stairs.

'We always keep our front door shut properly, don't we?' Gabrielle said to her mother.

There was no knocker and the bell didn't work.

'Our front door bell works, doesn't it?' Gabrielle said. She began to wonder if she really wanted to stay here. Her mother tapped on the door with her painted fingernails.

'They might all be away,' said Gabrielle. Her mother looked so stunning in her glittering dress. Her father looked so grand in his evening suit. Gabrielle felt she might prefer to go to the opera with them.

'I don't want to stay here,' she said. She got ready to stamp her foot and put out her lower lip. But before she had time to start, Mrs Potter wandered along to the front door.

'Hello, darling!' said Gabrielle's mother to Mrs Potter. 'So here we are! And here's my little poppet, Gabrielle, for you! Must dash or we'll be so late! You know what it's like!'

Mrs Potter blinked and smiled slowly. Her brown apron was covered in flour and so were her hands.

'Goodbye, sweetie, have a simply lovely time!' said Gabrielle's mother.

'My father thinks they're going to miss the first act,' said Gabrielle. 'He hates being late for anything.'

Mrs Potter fluttered her hands in a vague welcome, so that the flour drifted down like snow. She had a vacant look, as though she was thinking about something far away. She said, 'The light is so pretty at this time in the evening, isn't it?' and she went on staring up at the sky.

'Where am I supposed to put my things? My father can't stand a cluttered hall,' said Gabrielle. 'When people come to visit us at our house, we hang up their coats in the cloakroom.' She looked round for a cloakroom, or some hooks. There were none. Instead, there was a heap of coats, and scarves, and anoraks and jackets, and boots, and one ballet shoe lying at the bottom of the stairs.

'Look, I've brought a strawberry gateau. It's got whipped double cream as well as buttercream, and lots of strawberries inside, and more on top. It's for your children's tea. My mother says they probably don't get strawberries very often, because of living in a town. I have strawberries whenever I want. We have a big strawberry garden, and a freezer.'

Mrs Potter held the carton for a moment, then put it down on a chair. There were, Gabrielle noticed, already a lot of other things piled on the chair, including books, a tennis racket, and a half-eaten cheese sandwich.

'We all love strawberries here,' said Mrs Potter. 'Yes, do put your things there.'

So Gabrielle put her case and her basket beside the heap on the floor. She laid her coat carefully on top. It was her best coat. At home, it had its own coat-hanger in the cloakroom.

'We have a person called Mrs Gale who comes in every day and makes our house nice and tidy,' said Gabrielle. 'You see, my father can't stand a mess.

15

And my mother's always busy, too, going out to see people. Haven't you got anybody?'

'Oh yes, we all lend a hand here. Everybody has their tasks,' said Mrs Potter. 'Why, that's new!' She glanced with interest at a messy patch of green and black scribbling on the wall. 'Benjy's work. What d'you suppose it is, Gabrielle? A hippo? Or a tractor? He does love drawing tractors.'

'Mrs Potter, don't you *mind* people scribbling on the walls?'

From the pram outside, came a roar like a hyena. The baby had tangled its feet in the straps as it tried to reach the last tin of baked beans at the end of its pram. Mrs Potter released it and carried it into the hall. She put it down while she brought in the pram. It crawled over to the coat pile, grunting like a pig as it went. Then it made a grab for the cake carton on the chair.

'I've never been in a family with a real baby before,' said Gabrielle. 'Can I play with it? I've got a baby doll at home called Daisy-Bright. She can do everything a real baby does, well most things, and I like playing with babies. Daisy-Bright has her own doll's crib and her own doll's bath.'

Gabrielle bent down to pick up the baby. The baby opened its mouth and bit Gabrielle's arm. Then it crawled away.

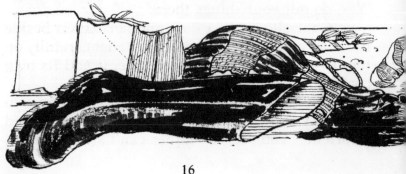

'Where are your *other* children, Mrs Potter?' Gabrielle asked. 'I think I'll go and play.'

'Children?' said Mrs Potter vaguely.

'I'd prefer to play with some of the older children,' said Gabrielle.

The pig-baby grabbed Gabrielle's new coat from the coat mound and dragged it along the floor in its teeth.

'They might be upstairs. I suppose. Benjy? Don? Charity? Matthew? Children? Where are you?' Mrs Potter called their names softly, as though she didn't really expect them to answer.

'Never mind,' said Gabrielle. 'I'll go and find them myself. You know, at home, my mother *always* knows exactly where I am, and what I'm doing. I suppose your children are playing Hide-and-Seek together, aren't they?'

'Well,' said Mrs Potter, 'I suppose Faith might be.' Slowly she gathered up the groceries from the pavement. 'Fancy that!' she said thoughtfully, looking with interest at the label on one of the tins.

## Chapter 4

Gabrielle set off up the stairs with her basket of things. She found Charity first. Charity was sitting on the bannisters making a noise like a horse.

'Hello, I'm Gabrielle. Are you Faith? I've come to stay here and be part of your family. I've always wanted to be part of a big family.'

Charity shook her head. 'No, Faith's upstairs. I'm Charity.'

'Well, I expect you're pleased to see me anyhow. I've brought all my best games and kits and I know lots of other games in my head. What shall we play first? Shall we play Hide-and-Seek?'

'I'm riding my horse at the moment. Maybe later.' She made horse-clopping noises.

'You haven't got any stirrups,' said Gabrielle. 'You can't ride without stirrups. On Thursdays I have riding lessons at a riding school on a real horse, so I know.'

'I'm Master of Hounds, so I'm allowed to ride this way,' said Charity. She made dog-barking noises. 'Those are all my foxhounds. We've got thirty in the pack. I'm very keen on bloodsports. Hey, Ryder! Joy! Heel, sir, heel, Barley!'

'I don't see any dogs.' said Gabrielle. All she could

see was some books stacked on the stairs. She put down her basket and took out the nurse's outfit. 'If you won't play Hide-and Seek, will you play Hospitals?'

Charity shook her head and made bugling noises. 'But Faith might,' she said. 'She likes that kind of thing better than me.'

Charity slid down from the bannisters and looked in Gabrielle's basket. She pulled out the miniature sewing-machine.

'That's nice. Could we do some sewing? I'd like to make a jacket for being Master of Hounds.'

Gabrielle put her sewing-machine back in her basket. 'No, you can't play with that. It's new. You might spoil it, and it's very difficult to get the thread sorted out if you tangle it up.'

Charity climbed back onto the bannisters and Gabrielle went on up the stairs. She found Faith sitting on the next landing with a tired, fat, black dog. Faith looked just the same as Charity, except that she had long red hair instead of short red hair.

'Gosh!' said Gabrielle. 'You're a twin! I've always wanted to have a twin. Why aren't you wearing the same clothes? Twins are supposed to, you know. I've got twin Dutch dolls and they always wear matching clothes. Will you come and play Hospitals?'

'Got to de-flea Punch,' said Faith. She tugged at the fat dog's black fur with a metal comb. She found a flea and she put it carefully into a bowl of water.

'Look at it swimming!'

'Our nextdoor neighbour's got a swimming pool,' said Gabrielle. 'I can do a back-flip off the board.'

'These fleas are so strong they could probably swim across the Channel and back.'

'It's not very kind to make them swim.'

20

'But *they're* not very kind to Punch. Anyway, I'll empty them onto the flowerbed in a minute. So they'll stand a sporting chance. You can help look for fleas if you like.' She handed Gabrielle the metal dog-comb.

'I think it's disgusting,' said Gabrielle. 'And *I* don't want to catch fleas.'

'Nor do I,' said Faith. 'But if we don't do it, then we'll *all* start to itch.'

'If you won't play Hospitals with me,' said Gabrielle, 'will you come and play charades? I brought my Disguise kit, with stick-on moustaches, and false eyebrows, and play make-up.'

Faith shook her head. 'It's my day to help lay the table. You can come and do it too if you like.'

'But I want to play!' said Gabrielle. 'I've come here specially to play games with all of you.'

'You could try the big ones,' said Charity. 'If you're not scared.'

'Scared of what? Why should I be?'

At that moment they heard loud noises of doors slamming, floors trembling, voices shouting and feet pounding. Gabrielle thought it sounded like people fighting, but Charity said it was only her brother Matt coming in and talking to Mrs Potter.

It was. They met him on the stairs as he hurtled up, two at a time.

'This the young visitor then?' he asked. 'Mum says she's got to be entertained.'

Matt had blue paint in his hair, and spattered on his glasses. He was very tall and when he peered down at her, Gabrielle felt rather short.

'Yes,' she said. 'I'm Gabrielle. I'm your visitor and I'd like to do some stencilling. Or else play charades, or snap, or blow football. Or anything you like.'

'Me and Don, we'll take you for a ride,' said Matt. 'If you're over six, and you promise not to scream, or cry, or fall off. And if you swear to do exactly what we tell you.'

'Of course I'm over six,' said Gabrielle grandly. 'And I *never* cry.'

'Come on then, hurry up. We haven't got all day.' Matt seized her hand and hurried her down to the front door so fast that she could hardly keep up.

'That's not fair!' Faith shouted after them. 'You never take *me* on your silly old cart.'

'You're not a visitor!' Matt shouted back. 'Anyway, we do.'

'Only sometimes.'

Don, the eldest of the Potter children, sat on the door-step reading a comic about alien space-monsters. He too had spots of blue paint on him. Matt gave him a nudge.

'Come on, dopey,' said Matt. 'Wake up. We're taking her for a quick spin on the chariot. Round the block.'

Don yawned as though he was exhausted and got up slowly. He bowed politely to Gabrielle.

'Gzam, gzat, grunch,' he said. 'Gy gam Gidon, the Gamma-eyed Gorilla, gat your gervice.'

The cart stood in the road. There was a lot of blue paint about, some on the cart, most on the ground. The cart was made from planks of wood, metal springs, and old pram wheels.

'Get on then,' said Matt. 'Only mind the paint.'

Gabrielle climbed on carefully, and sat down in the middle where it wasn't so wobbly.

'No,' said Matt. 'You have to lie down. Flat, on your front. Then you won't slip off when we're cornering.'

Don bowed again and rolled his eyes. 'Gamma-eyed Gidon grive you gnice gride.'

He and Matt took hold of the pulling rope at the front and set off at a rapid trot. The cart quickly gathered speed. The Potter's dog raced along behind, yapping.

Don and Matt went very fast so that the road and the lamp posts, the walls and the bushes rushed past in a coloured blur. Gabrielle held tightly on to the planks. She felt her stomach lurch sideways.

'You afraid of speed?' Matt turned and shouted.

'No, no, no,' Gabrielle shrieked back, 'not frightened,' even though she was.

The cart skidded round a corner on two wheels, and she thought she was going to slide off. Then it bumped over a track, plunged through a patch of mud sending up a brown spray on either side, swerved round the dog which had somehow got in front, and suddenly, they were back at the Potters' front door again and it was over.

Matt told her to get off. He and Don dragged the cart up into the hall. They thundered upstairs, jostling each other to be first.

'Is that all?' said Gabrielle. She followed them up, past Faith who was now de-fleaing the cat, past Charity riding the bannisters, past the pig-baby crawling along the passage dragging the yellow sponge-bag.

'That's mine. Give it back,' said Gabrielle and she snatched it from the baby's hand.

The doorway to the big boys' room was blocked by a pile of chairs, books and cardboard boxes balanced on top of each other. Don and Matt squirmed easily through a small gap which they blocked up after them with another cardboard box. Gabrielle peered through a chink into their room.

'Why won't you play any more?' she called.

'We *have* played,' said Matt.

'It wasn't very long,' said Gabrielle.

'Busy now,' said Matt. 'Got to paint the ceiling.'

Gabrielle saw him climb up onto the top bunkbed and start to paint the ceiling the same blue as the cart. The paint dribbled down his arms and onto his pillow.

'Gosh, are you allowed to?' she said. 'Ceilings are supposed to be white. Our ceilings at home are white. Two men came and did it when we were away on holiday. They wore overalls. You ought to wear an overall.'

'Don't shake the barricade please,' said Matt. 'It's there on purpose. To stop the baby getting in and mucking everything up.'

Gabrielle thought it looked pretty mucky already.

'If you stand still and don't touch or talk, you can watch,' said Matt.

'I don't want to just watch. I want to play.'

'Got to finish before supper,' said Matt.

Don wasn't painting. He was lying on the lower bunkbed reading his horror comic.

'*You*'re not busy,' said Gabrielle. 'Will you play some more?'

'Gidon Gamma-eyed Gorilla got glenty gomework,' said Don, tossing one comic under his bed and reaching for another.

'But you're not doing homework! You're just looking at comics!'

'Grunch, grunch, grunch, Gamma-eyed Gidon gmust gnow grest. Grery grery greghausted after glard glork glulling girl-gchild.' He rolled his eyes round, then pretended to go to sleep.

'You heard, Gabby,' said Matt. 'Off you trot, little dear. Why not try Benjy for a playmate? He's your best bet.'

'I don't *know* Benjy,' Gabrielle wailed. She put out her lower lip ready to cry. 'Nobody here's *any* good at playing properly.'

She wondered if it would be a good idea to have a scream and to stamp her feet like she sometimes did at home. She took a deep breath in readiness, but then decided that, as a visitor, she should set a good example. So, instead of screaming, she shouted through the barricade, 'I think you're the rudest boys I've ever met in my life! And anyway, my name's not Gabby. It's Gabrielle.'

Then she went off to look for Benjy.

## Chapter 5

Benjy was not in the Potters' living-room, though there were signs of wall-scribbling to show that, earlier, he might have been there. He was not in the hall, though there were signs here too, that he had been. Gabrielle went to the kitchen. Mrs Potter was pummelling a large sticky brown mass on the table.

'What's that?' Gabrielle asked. It looked like a wet slimy animal.

'Bread', said Mrs Potter. She smiled and went on pummelling.

'We don't do that to our bread at home,' said

26

Gabrielle. 'We fetch it from the freezer. It's wrapped in clean plastic bags.'

Mrs Potter thumped away with her fluttery hands, then broke a piece off, and offered it to Gabrielle to play with.

'No, thank you,' said Gabrielle.

Benjy was in the backyard, washing a tricycle.

Gabrielle didn't want to play with him. He looked much too young. She had once had to play with a four-year-old before.

'I'm Gabrielle, and I'm a lot older than you, and I've come to stay,' Gabrielle told Benjy. 'I'd much rather play with the big ones, but they're all busy. I've brought my second-best tea-set, so we can play Mothers and Fathers. I'll be the mother, and you can be the baby.'

Benjy shook his head and went on rubbing the pedals of the tricycle with a yellow flannel which looked just like Gabrielle's except that it was covered in oil.

'Or noughts and crosses? I've got pencils.'

'Can't write yet,' said Benjy. 'Or read. I'll play Schools if you like. I'll be the teacher.'

'Don't be silly, you can't be teacher if you can't write,' said Gabrielle.

'I can,' said Benjy.

'I'll be teacher,' said Gabrielle. She took out her pencil case, her felt-tip pens, and her drawing book. She would put up with Benjy for the time being. 'Then *I* can teach *you* how to read,' she said.

Benjy shrugged, picked up the yellow flannel and went on rubbing the pedals. 'I'll play if I can be the teacher and you be the schools people. You have to sit down there and do what I tell you.'

So Gabrielle sat down and put out her lower lip.

'Oh all right,' she said. 'But it's silly doing it this way.'

'No it isn't,' said Benjy.

They both tired of playing Schools, especially as Benjy didn't let Gabrielle have any turn at being teacher. She tidied her felt-tip pens and her pencils back into the pencil case.

'We could play Hairdressers?' said Benjy.

'But I haven't brought my dolls' Hair-Curl Set.'

'I've got things here,' said Bengy. 'I'll show you.'

He went indoors and came back with the metal dog-comb, and some water in a tooth mug, and a pair of nail clippers.

'I'm the hairdressing man and you're the person,' he said.

Gabrielle sat on the box. Benjy combed her fringe and her bunches with the comb.

'I've been to a proper salon with my mother,' said Gabrielle. 'And they don't do it like that. They don't pull and hurt.'

'All right, I won't play if you don't want me to.'

'I *do* want to. Only don't keep hurting,' said Gabrielle.

Benjy dabbed water onto one of Gabrielle's bunches then clipped the ends off with the nail clippers.

Gabrielle looked at the cut ends of her hair on the ground. She wasn't sure what to say. Nobody had played this sort of game with her before. She decided to sob. She sobbed and sobbed so much that Charity poked her head out of one of the upstairs windows, and then came down to have a closer look. Faith poked her head out of the kitchen door and came and had a look too.

'I've done her a new hairdo!' said Benjy. 'She doesn't like it. She's crying.'

'He's cut it all off,' sobbed Gabrielle. It was nice having all three of them standing round her.

'Don't scream at him,' said Faith. 'He's only little.'

'She asked me to do it. We were playing Hairdressers,' said Benjy. He wandered away and began to snip the petals off the marigolds.

'He ought to be spanked,' sobbed Gabrielle.

'If you *ask* somebody to do something, you can't be surprised if they go and do it,' said Faith.

Charity gathered up Gabrielle's hair.

'You can take it home and use it,' she said. 'There's lots of different things you can do with hair.' She put the hair into Gabrielle's basket. 'I put some on my bear who was bald. And you can make cushions with it, and Charity put some in her scrapbook.'

'And you can put it down people's necks to make them itch,' said Benjy. Then he went indoors with a piece of green chalk, and Faith went in to finish laying the table, and Charity went in to help her because Faith said she was getting in such a muddle about which side the forks go.

Gabrielle unpacked her Nurse kit and played Hospitals all on her own, just like she did at home. She pretended she was in charge of twenty sick patients. She wished the Potters knew how to behave, and play normal games. She wished Mrs Potter would behave like the mother of a large family ought to, and organize the children into playing normally. She wished it would soon be suppertime. She wished it would be bedtime. She wished she had gone to the opera with her parents.

Then Charity came out with the cat. 'I've found you a patient,' she said.

'This isn't an animal's hospital,' said Gabrielle.

'Midge isn't an animal. She's a person and she's been injured in a terrible train accident and needs brain surgery,' said Charity. She took one of Gabrielle's play-bandages and began to bandage up the cat's head. Then she put the toy thermometer in the furry bit under the cat's front leg and pretended to take its temperature.

'The cat doesn't like it,' said Gabrielle. 'And I don't like the way you keep taking things out of my Junior Red Cross bag without asking me first. *I'm* the nurse and *I'm* wearing the uniform, so you have to ask *me* first.'

'I know *you're* the nurse. But *I'm* the consultant brain surgeon, so I'm important, and I can see that this cat needs an operation at once!'

'That's not the way *I* play Hospitals,' said Gabrielle. 'The way I play is the proper way, and its's always the person who wears the uniform who's the most important. And I'm a visitor here so you're meant to be nice to me.'

She took off the nurse's uniform, and put away all the Junior Red Cross kit equipment. She decided she liked the other twin better than Charity. She waited till Charity had gone away and then she unpacked her pocket calculator and played number games by herself.

It seemed a long time to wait before Charity came out again and told her that it was suppertime.

## Chapter 6

The family jostled and shoved round the table trying to make room for each other. The pig-baby was put in a high chair which it kept trying to climb out of, but nobody else had a particular place of their own. Don fetched two more chairs from the bedroom barricade.

'At home,' said Gabrielle, 'my father always sits at the end of the table, and my mother sits the other end and I sit in the middle. We sit in the same places every day and then we don't get in a muddle.'

Nobody heard what Gabrielle did at home because they were busy talking and trying to count how many more chairs were needed. Matt fetched a stool but there still didn't seem to be enough places. Mrs Potter and Benjy fetched two more plates. Benjy dropped his. The baby beat its tin dish with a spoon. Faith leapt across from her stool onto a chair, pretending to be an acrobat. Charity crawled under the table growling and said she was a sick dog. Don came down still pretending to be a gorilla and tried to sit down where there wasn't a chair. He fell backwards onto the floor. The Potters thought it was very funny, so he did it again.

'I don't think that's very funny,' said Gabrielle.

When everybody was finally sitting down, they still went on talking and clattering their plates and noisily passing the salt and the pepper, and the water jug and pieces of bread this way and that, up and down the table.

'But what about your father?' said Gabrielle.

'What?' said Charity.

'Your Daddy.'

'Oh him!' said Charity. 'Can I have the bread, please?'

'Don't you wait for him to get home before you start?'

'He doesn't live here any more.'

Gabrielle wondered why not. Perhaps he didn't like the noise.

The Potters' stew was thick and chunky and the bread was brown and lumpy. So was the rice. The vegetables were in big chopped-up raw chunks. Gabrielle chewed and chewed. It looked like the kind of food that Gabrielle's mother bought for Gabrielle to give to her rabbit.

The baby ate with its hands and scattered crumbs. Mrs Potter, who now had a ruffled look as though she had only just got out of bed, sat next to the baby and occasionally puts bits of food into its mouth.

'My rabbit's a very tidy eater,' said Gabrielle. 'It doesn't make any mess.'

'Yuk, yukkity,' said Faith. She was sitting next to Gabrielle. 'Yukkity, brown, brown, brown.' Faith ate her bread but left the rest of her food.

'If you don't like this kind of food, why does Mrs Potter give it to you?' Gabrielle asked. '*My* mother gives me what I like for supper, not what I hate. She asks me what I want and then, if I say fish fingers and chips and no tomato, she gives it to me. And if I say chicken and ice-cream, then she gives me that.'

'Our Ma says chewing's good for the digestion,' said Faith.

Matt reached across the table and scooped up the food which Faith had left on her plate.

'If *you're* not hungry, I certainly am!' he said.

Nobody in Gabrielle's dining room ever reached across the table and helped themselves to bits of food off each other's plates. Even Gabrielle's rabbit had its own cabbage.

Gabrielle swallowed her brown food quickly so that there would be nothing for Matt to take. The Potters seemed to be a very hungry family. Even Faith who said 'Yukkity-yuk', after every mouthful, ate four slices of bread. Soon there was only brown crumbs, a dribble of brown stew, and a sliver of grated cabbage left. Gabrielle thought about the strawberry gateau. Had Mrs Potter forgotten it?

At home, Gabrielle's father said it was bad manners for children to get up in the middle of meals. But the Potters got up and down all the time. So Gabrielle got up too and went to the hall. The cake-carton was still on the chair where Mrs Potter had left it, only now it was hidden underneath everything else. The lid was dented. The cream whirls were flattened.

'Strawberry cake! Yum!' said Faith.

'It's called gateau,' said Gabrielle.

'Clever girl, Gabby,' said Mrs Potter. 'I'd never have remembered.'

'At home my mother always writes important things down on the memo-board,' said Gabrielle, 'She never forgets anything.'

She put the gateau in the middle of the Potter's table. When she had been holding it in the back of the sports car it had seemed a very large gateau. Now, beside the Potters' big black stew pot, and the Potters' big bread board, and with all the Potters themselves around the table, it seemed a very small gateau indeed. Gabrielle hoped the baby would not be given too much. Being a baby, it might not be given any at all. This would be best. But, being the youngest, it might get the largest slice of all, as she did at home.

Gabrielle hoped that Mrs Potter would be fair about cutting, so that everybody would receive the same sized piece.

'At home, my mother always shares things absolutely fairly, into three portions,' she said.

Matt fetched a knife, but he didn't give it to Mrs Potter. He handed it to Faith.

'Why's Faith cutting it?' Gabrielle asked Charity, who was sitting on the other side of her.

'Fair shares,' said Charity. 'Her turn. Well, she *says* it is, because *she* laid the table. But *I* don't think she laid it very well, so *I* don't think it is her turn. I think it's mine because I de-flead Punch.'

They both watched Faith carefully.

'It must be awful only having the nice things when it's your turn,' said Gabrielle.

'It is. You wait and wait, and sometimes you miss your turn because you're doing something else,' said Charity.

Faith did not divide the gateau fairly. It was a squishy gateau. The knife was not sharp. Faith could not have cut it fairly even if she had been trying. Gabrielle decided that, after all, maybe she preferred Charity to Faith.

Faith handed round the slices. Charity and Gabrielle did not get a strawberry at all on their pieces. Matt had three on his. Mrs Potter's slice was all whipped cream and no sponge. Don's was all sponge, with only half a blob of one of the squashed cream whirls. He didn't seem to mind, but just smiled, and made a dopey face, and said, 'Me Gidon-Gorilla gike gake.'

'It isn't *really* fair to let a child share out a gateau,' said Gabrielle. 'It's best if a grown-up does it.'

The baby wiped cream in its hair.

'If you came and stayed again, would you bring another cake?' asked Benjy. He had the largest slice of all.

'Of course she would,' said Faith.

'I hope you come again then,' said Benjy.

'My teacher at school,' said Gabrielle, 'says you should like people for what they are, not for what they give you.'

*Chapter 7*

After supper, Don carried the baby up to bed on his
shoulder and Mrs Potter put the lead on to the dog
and took it out. Then, Charity, Faith and Benjy
cleared the table while Matt bossed them about.
Gabrielle watched. Benjy dropped a mug and two
forks. Matt piled up six plates with a butter dish on

38

top to show how it should be done and didn't drop a thing.

'At home,' said Gabrielle, 'my mother doesn't let me carry things to the dishwasher in case I break the best china.'

But the Potters didn't have a dishwasher. They argued about whose turn it was to wash up. They all said it was Don's turn but he was putting the baby to bed. So Matt said he'd do it. He squirted so much detergent into the sink that froth foamed up over the top. He splashed water everywhere, especially over the cat. Nobody seemed to mind.

Matt sang *Good King Wenceslas* very loudly while he dried up, and he flicked his drying-up cloth at Faith and told her she wasn't doing her drying-up properly. Faith flicked her drying-up cloth back at him. Gabrielle began to wish that she had a drying-up cloth to flick too, but by then they had finished.

Mrs Potter came back with the dog. She cooked meat for the dog's supper, and fishheads for the cat, and didn't notice the water all over the floor. She said thank you to everybody for clearing away, even to Gabrielle who hadn't done any. Then she kissed them all and said that it was time for all those who had no homework to go to bed.

'Where am I sleeping?' asked Gabrielle. 'We have a special room at home called the guest room with a pink carpet.'

'You'll manage to squeeze Gabby in somewhere, won't you children?' said Mrs Potter with a smile. 'There's always room for one more little one.'

'She can have *my* bed,' said Matt. 'I prefer the floor.'

'She's sleeping in with *us*,' said Faith.

Gabrielle fetched her vanity case and followed the others upstairs. The dog and the cat went with them.

'Doesn't Mrs Potter *take* you up to bed?' Gabrielle said. 'At home my mother always *takes* me to bed.'

'What for?' Faith asked. 'Can't you undo buttons for yourself and clean your own teeth? Even Benjy can undress himself.'

'Course I can,' said Gabrielle. 'But my mother sits in the bathroom and talks to me.'

'We'll talk,' said Benjy.

'Then afterwards she reads me a bedtime story. I can't get to sleep unless I have a story. And when my mother goes out, my babysitter reads me a story.'

'We have a bedtime story too,' said Faith. 'We read it ourselves. And Benjy listens because he can't read words. And tonight *I'm* reading it.'

'No you aren't,' said Charity.

'Am,' said Faith.

'Are not,' said Charity. 'You did it yesterday. It's my turn tonight.'

'All right. But my turn to choose,' said Faith.

'I'm not reading some grotty old book *you've* chosen,' said Charity.

'Don't then. I'll choose a book and read it myself,' said Faith.

Gabrielle was glad that she didn't have a twin sister. At home, *she* always chose which story she wanted read.

'Crumbs, look at Gabby's pyjamas!' said Faith suddenly.

'Ooh, lovely! All frilly. I wish I had pyjamas like that,' said Charity. 'Do a swap, Gabby?' She fetched her pyjamas out of a cardboard box which was painted to look like a dolls' house.

'I've never swapped pyjamas before,' said Gabrielle. She didn't like the sound of it.

'Please?' said Faith.

'Please, please?' said Charity. 'Just for one night? They're so pretty.'

Gabrielle thought her pyjamas were pretty too and she didn't like the look of Faith's pyjamas which were old and faded, and dull and striped.

'Give you my best rubber band,' said Faith, taking it out of her pocket.

'And I'll give you my best animal,' said Charity, searching under her pillow, and handing Gabrielle a yellow plastic giraffe. Gabrielle knew it came free out of a cereal packet.

Faith and Charity shared Gabrielle's pyjamas between them. Charity took the top half, Faith took the legs. Gabrielle had to put on Faith's faded pair.

'They're too big for me,' said Gabrielle.

Faith nodded. 'I know! They're too big for me too,' she said.

'And they're *boys'* pyjamas!' said Gabrielle.

'Course they are. Passed on from Matt. All our clothes are boys'. If Matt had been a girl called Matilda, and Don had been a girl called Donna, I expect we'd wear *girls'* clothes all the time.'

Faith and Charity danced round the beds and crashed into the baby's cot.

'I want a swap too,' said Benjy.

'No, get into bed. Three people can't share one pair of pyjamas,' said Faith, but Charity looked in Gabrielle's case.

'Ooh, look at this lovely material!' she said, pulling out Gabrielle's green velvet dress.

'I'd rather you didn't take it out,' said Gabrielle. 'It's my special dress.'

41

'That's why I thought you'd want to share it.'

'I don't want to wear a girl's dress,' said Benjy.

'You could lend him this nice dressing-gown?' said Charity.

Gabrielle grabbed it back. 'I'd rather not,' she said. 'He's already got my flannel. I don't lend my clothes.'

'We do, all the time,' said Faith. 'He wouldn't hurt it, would you Benjy? Just wear it.'

Benjy pulled the dressing-gown on over his pyjamas. It was too long for him. He took it off and draped it over his head like a cloak, then he climbed into bed.

'People don't get into bed *in* their dressing-gowns,' said Gabrielle.

'Don't they?' said Faith. 'What are they for then?'

'I wear mine when I'm walking along the passage.'

'Where to?'

'From my bathroom to my bedroom, of course. So I won't catch a chill.'

She wished she was at home now, walking along the passage to her own bedroom. Her mother would hang her dressing-gown neatly on the hook behind her door, and fold back the bedspread and Gabrielle would climb into her own bed. Here, she didn't seem to have a bed at all, and Benjy was crumpling her dressing-gown by lying down in it.

'Come head-to-toes with me,' said Charity. 'You wouldn't want to share with Faith because she kicks about, and Benjy snores, and Sybil's cot's so damp.'

Gabrielle wondered what head-to-toes was. She didn't think it sounded very nice. Charity showed her.

'You get in the proper end and when I've untucked this end, I get in. Then we lie down.'

When they were in, they each had the other's toes

beside their ears. Charity tickled Gabrielle's toes. Then Charity wriggled her own toes against Gabrielle's bunches. 'It's nice like this,' Charity said. 'You don't get lonely. And you won't miss having your mother talking to you.'

Faith got a book and began to read the bedtime story. Benjy and Gabrielle listened and Charity began to listen and suddenly remembered she had said she wouldn't, so she hummed to herself.

Gabrielle wished that Mrs Potter had come up to read the story like a proper mother, for Faith was not a good reader. She stumbled over words. She mispronounced them. She left out bits of sentences so that the book didn't make sense. And the book she'd chosen wasn't even a proper story. It was a list of facts about cars and car engines. Benjy didn't seem to mind but Gabrielle was glad when the reading was over. Charity came out from under the blanket and stopped humming and she and Faith talked about how far open the door should be, and how much the curtains should be drawn.

Faith wanted the door wide open. Charity wanted it closed. Faith wanted the curtains quite shut, Charity wanted them open.

'So that we we can see the morning sun,' she said.

They argued some more, then decided to have the door halfway, and to have the curtain nearest to Faith drawn, and the one nearest to Charity open. Benjy wasn't allowed to say which he wanted. Nor was Gabrielle.

At home, Gabrielle did not like to see the curtains pulled different amounts. Her mother had to get them exactly the same. She had to get the door open exactly the right amount too, so that the light from the passage shone into Gabrielle's room but not onto her face, otherwise Gabrielle moaned instead of going to sleep.

Tonight, she did not think she would ever fall asleep. The light from the half-open door shone right across her face, and Charity's wriggling toes lay on the pillow beside her ear. And the dog, stretched on the floor under Benjy's bed, thumped its tail. The cat curled itself up on Charity's half of the bed, so that Gabrielle couldn't move her own legs properly. The baby snuffled in its cot. Don and Matt in the next room made thudding noises like a pillow fight, and Faith's bed-springs creaked. Benjy fell asleep with his mouth wide open and snored. Faith crawled to the end of her bed, and reached over to close Benjy's mouth. But it didn't make any difference.

Then, from downstairs came another noise.

'What is it?' Gabrielle whispered.

'You mean that sound like a mouse squeaking?' whispered Charity.

'Yes,' said Gabrielle.

'And like an elephant moaning?' whispered Faith.

'Yes.' said Gabrielle.

'It's music,' said Faith. 'Isn't it lovely? Ma plays her music after we've gone to bed. Like an animal lullaby.'

'To send us to sleep,' added Charity.

'But doesn't she come and tuck you up and kiss you goodnight?'

'Of course. But not yet. Not till we're properly asleep, or nearly properly.'

'My mother tucks me up as *soon* as I'm in bed.'

'What if you have to get up again for something? Then the tucking up and kissing's all wasted,' said Faith.

'Then I call her back and she comes up and does it again,' said Gabrielle.

'Our mother only does it once,' said Faith.

## Chapter 8

When Gabrielle woke, the Potters' house was all quiet, except for a loud gnawing noise.

Sleeping head-to-toes was not, Gabrielle realized, nearly as bad as she had expected. Then, she saw that she was not head-to-toes any more. Charity was on the floor, wrapped round in a blanket like a sausage roll. Faith was asleep, too. So was Benjy. The gnawing noise was the baby, standing in its cot, chewing the bars. The baby saw Gabrielle looking at it and gurgled.

'Sssh!' said Gabrielle. She crept out of bed and along the passage. She was hungry. She wanted to see if Mrs Potter was getting the breakfast. As she started down the stairs, the baby screamed. Gabrielle went back into the bedroom.

'I said ssh!' she said, but again, as she started to go out of the room, the baby screamed. Next it rocked its cot. It rocked so much that the cot jerked forward like a stiff animal walking. The baby looked more than ever like a pig this morning with its face red from screaming, and its nose flattened from pressing against the cot bars. So long as it could see Gabrielle it grunted and gnawed. As soon as Gabrielle was out of sight, it screamed and jerked.

Gabrielle tried three times to leave the room. Three times, the baby screamed and rocked. Scream, shake, jerk, scream, shake, jerk. The baby made it seem as though it was Gabrielle's fault that it was screaming. Yet Gabrielle was sure it wasn't. Gabrielle wondered how Benjy, Faith, and Charity could sleep through the noise.

'All right, piglet, you'll have to come too.' Crossly, she pulled the baby out of its cot. It was heavier than she expected and she dropped it. It didn't seem to mind but picked itself up and toddled towards the stairs. Gabrielle followed.

Mrs Potter was not in the kitchen making breakfast. Nobody was. The whole house was silent except for the dog whining at the back door. Gabrielle let it out and it ran round the backyard barking, then came in and wagged its tail at her. The

47

baby crawled under the kitchen table and found a fish-bone in the cat's bowl. Gabrielle picked it up and heaved it into its highchair. Then she looked for some food for it.

She found a jar of plum jam and a packet of digestive biscuits. She mixed them together on a saucer and fed them to the baby with a teaspoon just as she fed Daisy-Bright. The baby opened its mouth for more, which was more fun than Daisy-Bright. Then the baby grasped the jam-pot and threw it on the floor, which was less fun than Daisy-Bright, so Gabrielle stopped playing with it and fetched her dot-to-dot drawing book, and did dot-to-dot drawing until Matt came down. He was singing *On Top of Old Smokey* and he wasn't as grumpy as the day before.

'Top o' the morning to you, Gabby,' he said.

'My name's not Gabby. It's Gabrielle. I keep telling everybody.'

'Never mind. We can't all be perfect.' And he set about breakfast. First, he cooked porridge for the baby. Then he mixed a jug of hot chocolate, and a bowl of batter.

'How many pancakes can you eat? I'm having five.'

'I've never heard of people eating *pancakes* for breakfast,' said Gabrielle. She didn't want her breakfast cooked by a boy. She wanted an adult, preferably a mother adult, to come down and cook it, the way mothers should.

'Why isn't your mother coming down?' she said.

'It's her lie-in,' said Matt. He tried to toss one of the pancakes. It landed on the floor. He called the dog over to eat it.

'Want a fried egg on top, Gabby?' he asked.

'I've never heard of people eating *eggs* with pancakes,' said Gabrielle.

He told her to carry the baby into the backyard, and he'd bring the pancakes.

'And I've never heard of people eating their breakfast out of doors,' Gabrielle said. But the smell of fried pancakes was so good that she couldn't help wanting to eat one. She sat on an empty wooden crate, and Matt sat on another, and the baby sat on the ground, and Gabrielle ate three pancakes with fried eggs on top, two pancakes with maple syrup, and one pancake with both. She drank two mugs of hot chocolate.

When the other children came down, in ones and twos, Matt cooked more pancakes. He didn't get red in the face and cross like Gabrielle's mother did, once a year on Shrove Tuesday. He sang, and fried, and after twenty-six pancakes, was even quite good at tossing them. When all the children were full up, and the dog had been given the last cold congealed pancake, Matt said, 'Now we'll play!'

The Potters all ran into the living-room. Don put on a record of music very loudly and Matt took off his glasses and put them on the bookshelf. Then the children hurled themselves onto the floor in a writhing heap.

'What are you doing?' Gabrielle shrieked.

'Playing our game,' said Faith.

'It doesn't look like playing. It looks like fighting,' said Gabrielle. 'What are the rules?'

'There aren't any. You just join in whenever you want, only you have to take off your shoes first if you're wearing them. And your glasses, if you've got glasses. Come on, Gabby, it's lovely!'

Faith was still on top of the heap. Another person,

who looked as though she might have been Charity, was at the bottom. The baby joined in, toddling round the edge, bleating like a goat, and grabbing at any leg, hand, or bunch of hair that it could reach. Benjy crawled out from the bottom of the heap. He wasn't laughing any more.

'Poor little Benjy,' said Gabrielle. 'Look, you lot, you've made him cry.'

Nobody took any notice of Gabrielle or Benjy, and after a moment Benjy wiped his eyes and threw himself back into the muddle.

'It's the silliest game I've *ever* seen!' Gabrielle shouted. '*And* dangerous! And I'm going to go and tell Mrs Potter.'

She ran upstairs to Mrs Potters' bedroom. Mrs Potter was sitting up in bed drinking tea and

reading a book. The Potter childrens' shrieking and yelping downstairs, was very loud but Mrs Potter didn't seem to hear.

'Yes, it's very silly of them, isn't it, Gabrielle?' she agreed and went on reading.

'They're not even dressed yet. And they'll get hurt,' said Gabrielle.

'Yes, I expect one of them will,' said Mrs Potter. 'They usually do.'

Gabrielle went downstairs. She wished it was time to go home.

'I think Gabby wants to play too,' said Charity. Her head was sticking out of the huddle, and her legs were tangled up with somebody else's. There was a muffled crack from the middle of the heap, like a twig breaking. Charity squealed.

'Crikes,' said Matt. 'Breaking limbs. Better call it off.' He pulled himself out of the heap and put on his glasses.

'It's me,' said Charity. She staggered to her feet, clutching her hand. 'My finger. Somebody bent it back and stood on it.'

Don put Charity's finger into a sink of cold water and made funny faces to cheer her up. It didn't make any difference. Her hand swelled up. They all went up to tell Mrs Potter.

'Sorry, Ma, I think we've hurt Charity's finger,' said Matt.

Mrs Potter sighed, and got out of bed. She didn't seem angry. 'Maybe I'll have to take her along to Casualty,' she said. 'As soon as I've had some coffee.'

'If somebody broke *my* hand,' Gabrielle said to Faith, 'I'd be very upset.'

'It's not her hand. It's only her little finger.'

'I'd still want them to be spanked and put to bed.'

52

'Why? Nobody did it on purpose,' said Faith. 'It was just as much her fault. She didn't *have* to play, did she?'

Gabrielle went upstairs to dress, and to pack her things. She found her best green dress draped over a chair where Charity had been trying it on. She found her fluffy blue dressing-gown halfway down Benjy's bed with his teddy wrapped inside it. She found her coat in the coat heap and her yellow face-flannel, all grimy, in the garden. Then she went and found Mrs Potter.

Mrs Potter was staring out of a window with the baby in her arms. 'Aren't those clouds such a pretty shape?' she said.

'I've packed my things,' said Gabrielle. 'Is it time for me to go home yet?'

'Home?' said Mrs Potter. 'Oh yes, of course. Quite soon.'

'Is my mother coming to fetch me? Or my father?' Gabrielle hoped it would be her father in the sports car. On the other hand, if it was her mother, they would probably go to the shops and perhaps buy a new toy.

'We're taking you home, Gabby dear,' said Mrs Potter. 'Your mother's invited us to coffee.'

'*All* of you?' said Gabrielle. 'At *my* house?' She could not imagine the Potters coming to her home.

## Chapter 9

The Potters had a blue van which smelled, even before you got in, of something strong.

'Fish,' said Faith. 'It used to belong to a fishmonger. He drove about selling fish in boxes of ice. Then he got a new refrigerated van. So he sold us this one.'

'Not sold,' said Faith. 'Gave.'

'He didn't give it. He sold it in exchange for one of Ma's weavings.'

'That's not selling. That's bartering.'

'All right then. He bartered.'

Gabrielle could see it must be the worst thing in the world to have a twin sister who contradicted everything you said.

The Potters kept their van standing under a lamp-post at the top of a slope two streets away. Matt explained that they had to keep it there, otherwise it wouldn't start.

'We keep our cars in the garage at home,' said Gabrielle.

'Ma needs the slope because of the battery. It's flat,' said Faith.

'It isn't the battery. It's the plugs,' said Matt.

'When our car didn't work, my father rang up the factory. They sent a mechanic to our house,' Gabrielle said.

Mrs Potter got into the driver's seat. Matt, Don, Faith, and Gabrielle went behind the van to push. Charity ran too but because of her hand being bandaged and her arm in a sling, she couldn't really push at all. She just got in everybody's way. They ran and ran. Then the van made a bang like a gun, and suddenly lurched away from the children, so that Faith fell over in the road and Gabrielle fell on top of her. Faith grazed her elbow. Gabrielle cut her knee. The van moved forward with only Mrs Potter in it. It went faster and faster down the hill, then disappeared round a corner. Matt cheered and Don beat his chest with his fists like a happy gorilla.

Gabrielle looked at the blood trickling down her leg. She wanted to open her mouth and howl. She wanted to be carried back to the house. She wanted a lollipop to make it better. She wanted somebody to make a fuss of her.

'Here, Gabs. Have this hanky,' said Matt and he wrapped it around Gabrielle's knee, and gave her a pat on the shoulder. 'Brave old thing,' he said.

Charity took off her sling and gave it to Faith for her grazed elbow. Then the van, with Mrs Potter in it, reappeared. They climbed into the back and drove to the Potter's front door to collect Benjy and the baby. It didn't seem as though there could be room for anybody else. But there was still the dog to be squeezed in, as well as Mrs Potter's harvest loaf shaped like a plait and sprinkled with poppy seeds.

The fish-van ground slowly forwards. Inside it was noisy and cramped. Benjy squashed up against Gabrielle, and Faith's knee dug into her back. Her case and her basket poked into her ankle bones. The dog leaned against her back and panted with its wet tongue lolling out. The baby crawled over everybody.

The Potters didn't mind being squashed. And they didn't mind not having proper seats, except Don who was allowed to sit in front as he was the eldest.

Matt sang *O, We Do Like To Be Beside the Sea-side* very loudly.

'But we're nowhere near the sea,' said Gabrielle.

'He always sings that, because of the smell of the fish,' said Faith.

Benjy said, 'I feel sick!'

'I do too,' said Faith.

Gabrielle felt sick but she didn't say anything.

Mrs Potter told Don to hand round the toffee tin.

'Molasses stops nausea,' she said.

The toffee was treacle-flavoured in black sticky squares. Benjy took the largest piece, and as soon as he was tired of it, he took it out of his mouth and gave it to Gabrielle.

'I don't want it,' she said. 'I've got a piece.'

Benjy put it down on Gabrielle's skirt. Gabrielle glared at Benjy, and nudged him in the ribs. Then she picked the toffee off her skirt and held it between her fingers. The dog leaned over and began to lick it.

Suddenly, through the misted-up window, Gabrielle saw her own village looking friendly and familiar.

'Look! It's my village!' she said. 'And my post office! And there's my riding-stables! And my sweet-shop! And there's my neighbour with the swimming-pool.'

Mrs Potter turned in through the white gates. The van spluttered down the drive. Gabrielle peered past Benjy's ear and round Charity's shoulder.

'And there's my house.' Her climbing-frame was still on the lawn, and her swing. Everything was in its proper place as it should be. Gabrielle felt she had been away for a long time.

'What a terrific house. Let's explore!' said Faith. They scrambled out of the van and raced in through the front door. Gabrielle didn't wait to be kissed by her mother. She ran after the Potter children.

'Please don't,' she begged the children. 'Please don't *play* anything.'

Matt, Don, and the dog rushed up the stairs. Faith opened a door that wasn't meant to be opened. She climbed into a cupboard that wasn't meant to be climbed into. Benjy scrambled over the arm-chairs and slid down the bannisters. Charity took down

twenty-nine of the fifty-four board games from their tidy places on the playroom shelf.

'What a lot of toys you've got,' she said.

'Please,' said Gabrielle, 'don't.'

The baby found the jig-saws and threw handfuls of pieces into the air like confetti. Faith ran upstairs to Gabrielle's bedroom. She thumbed through the books, and left them higgledy-piggledy on the shelf with the pages turned back.

'What a lot of books you've got, Gabby!' she said.

Benjy took Gabrielle's seventeen dolls down from the doll-shelf, undressed them, and put them into the bath.

'What a lot of dolls!' he said. 'Look, they're at the seaside!' He sprayed them with the shower.

'We do like your house, Gabby. Smasho-terrif!' said Matt. 'Can we see the garden?' He dashed past her with the badminton set. The others followed.

Benjy and Charity rolled in Gabrielle's father's hedge-trimmings. Then they threw them at each other.

'Please,' said Gabrielle. 'The mess.'

Don climbed the apple tree, and swung from a branch by one arm.

'You're meant to climb on the climbing-frame!' Gabrielle screamed. 'Not the tree. You'll make the leaves fall off.'

Benjy fetched Gabrielle's portable television from her bedroom and took it into the tree-house. Charity found Gabrielle's green bicycle and wheeled it out onto the lawn. But with her broken finger, she steered into a flowerbed and fell off into a clump of dahlias. Matt practised long jumps in the sand-pit. The baby paddled in the goldfish pool and tried to drink the water.

At last, it was time for the Potters to go away. Mrs Potter waved her pale hands and softly called the children's names. Reluctantly they appeared. Then Don remembered the dog.

At last all the Potters and their dog were packed into their smelly van and grinning through the windows. With a weak juddering, the van lurched forward and the Potters were gone.

## Chapter 10

Gabrielle hurried upstairs to her bedroom. First, she picked up all her books; then she rearranged her toys as they should be, in order of size. Then she straightened her bedcovers. Then, humming to herself, she fished her dolls out of the bath, dried them, dressed them, and put them tidily back on their shelf. Then she changed out of the skirt which Benjy had made sticky with treacle-toffee, and which Faith had spilled milk on. Then she put on her green velvet dress with the muslin collar, and she put on a frilly petticoat underneath, and she brushed her hair so that the cut bit on one side hardly showed at all. Then she admired herself in the mirror, and finally, she went downstairs to her mother.

'Poppet darling, there you are!' said her mother.

Gabrielle did a little twirl on one leg so that her skirts and her curls swirled out.

'You do look a pretty moppet today,' said her mother. 'And did you have a marvellous time? Aren't they such a lovely family? I knew you'd get on. And dear Mrs Potter says you can stay there again any time!'

'No thank you, mummy dear,' said Gabrielle. 'I'd much rather kind Mrs Brown came and babysat me here.'

'Precious, are you sure?'

Gabrielle nodded. 'I don't mind how often you have to go out, because I know I'm the happiest, luckiest girl in the world living here with just Daddy and you, and the rabbit.'